Emma Thomson's felicity Wishes®

Party Pickle

and other stories

Hodder Children's Books

A division of Hachette Children's Books

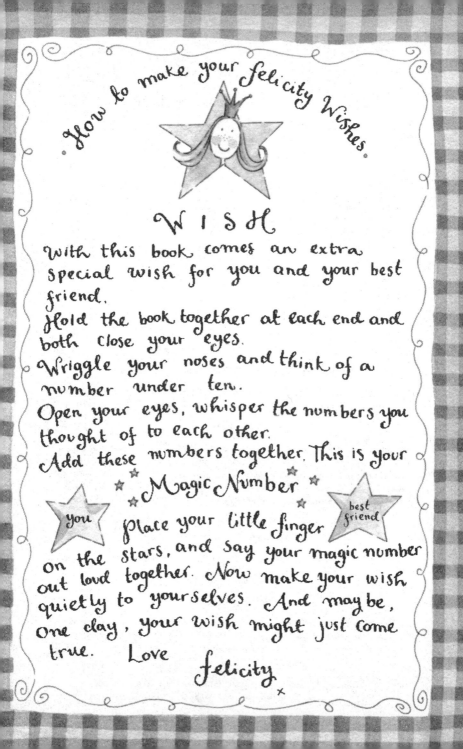

How to make your felicity Wishes

W I S H

With this book comes an extra special wish for you and your best friend.

Hold the book together at each end and both close your eyes.

Wriggle your noses and think of a number under ten.

Open your eyes, whisper the numbers you thought of to each other.

Add these numbers together. This is your

Magic Number

you

best friend

place your little finger on the stars, and say your magic number out loud together. Now make your wish quietly to yourselves. And maybe, one day, your wish might just come true. Love

felicity

x

For Molly Tattersall
with love from Auntie Emma

FELICITY WISHES
Felicity Wishes © 2000 Emma Thomson
Licensed by White Lion Publishing

Text and Illustrations © 2005 Emma Thomson

First published in Great Britain in 2005 by Hodder Children's Books

The right of Emma Thomson to be identified as the author and illustrator of this work has
been asserted by her in accordance with the Copyright, Designs and Patents Act 1988.

3

A Catalogue record for this book is available from the British Library

ISBN: 978 0 340 90245 5

Printed in China.

The paper and board used in this paperback by Hodder Children's Books are natural recyclable
products made from wood grown in sustainable forests. The manufacturing processes
conform to the environmental regulations of the country of origin.

Hodder Children's Books
A division of Hachette Children's Books, 338 Euston Road, London NW1 3BH
An Hachette Livre UuK Company

CONTENTS

Glittering Gems

"Why so glum?" enquired Polly, spotting Felicity's unhappy expression. "Are you upset that the school play is over?"

"Yes." Felicity nodded sadly.

"Me too," said Holly, slumping down beside Felicity. "I was getting quite used to being the centre of attention."

The School of Nine Wishes had just finished a three-day run of its annual school play and Holly had performed the main role brilliantly.

Felicity had been one of the chorus and even though she hadn't had any lines to read, she had loved every moment of the experience.

"I'm really going to miss my costume," said Felicity, looking down at her own dress which looked dowdy by comparison. "Every time I put it on, I felt like a star with all those sequins and glitter."

"Well, you were a star!" said Holly, who meant it quite literally.

In the closing scene, Felicity, Polly, Daisy and the rest of the cast had worn beautiful golden outfits in the shape of stars. While they hovered against a purple velvet backdrop, Holly had sung her solo centre-stage. The effect had been so magical that the crowd had clapped for an encore every single night.

"When are we ever going to get dressed up like that again?" sighed Felicity.

"Well," whispered Polly excitedly, "Fairy Godmother is already planning next year's play."

"Next year!" burst out Felicity. "I can't wait a whole year!"

"Well, you can't start coming to school in sequins and glitter!" said Holly, reading her friend's mind.

Felicity frowned.

"I know!" she said, suddenly springing to her feet. "I'll have a fancy dress party! Then we can wear anything we like! The more outrageous the better!"

Holly groaned quietly under her breath. Fancy dress parties were her worst nightmare; she always ended up looking silly rather than glamorous.

Without stopping to discuss the details, Felicity flew off to spread the exciting news to all her friends.

* * *

Felicity's fancy dress party was soon the talk of the school.

Felicity had stayed up all night making party invitations that boasted generous sprinklings of glitter. She had given them out to all her friends – and as Felicity was one of the friendliest fairies in Little Blossoming, that was a lot of fairies!

Invitation to Felicity's Fancy Dress Party
Theme – Nature

"And there's going to be a competition for the best outfit!" Felicity sang, handing out the last of the invitations to Holly, Polly and Daisy.

"What's the prize?" asked Holly curiously.

"A... um... um... secret surprise!" said Felicity, who hadn't actually thought of a prize yet.

"It's a bit of an odd theme," said Polly, inspecting her invitation.

"Nature?" said Daisy. "I think it's a lovely idea!" Daisy wanted to be a Blossom Fairy when she graduated from the School of Nine Wishes and knew instantly that her party outfit had to include flowers.

"You've just got to think a little creatively," Felicity explained to her friends. "Nature is all around us."

Holly wasn't convinced. To her, nature meant studying tadpoles in class or learning about the different types of trees in Nine Wish Wood.

Felicity could see that she was going to have to help her friends out a bit more.

"Look," she began, "tomorrow's Saturday. Why don't we all meet at my house? Then we can go for a nature walk for some inspiration."

Daisy jumped up and down at the idea but Holly still looked doubtful. If she was honest, she'd prefer to meet at Sparkles for a gossip and a giggle, but she knew how much it meant to Felicity that her party was a big success. So if that meant dressing up as a twig, Holly was reluctantly willing to give it a try.

✳ ✳ ✳

The next day everyone met bright and early at Felicity's house.

"Where shall we go?" asked Polly, who was always very sensible and liked to plan things properly.

"Nine Wish Wood!" suggested Daisy.

"Glitter Beach!" said Holly.

"Neither of those," said Felicity mysteriously. "You don't have to go very far to find nature. We're going to go somewhere where we'll find more ideas for fancy dress outfits than we'll know what to do with!" With a smile, she opened her back door.

"My back garden!"

Holly groaned quietly to herself.

"Right!" said Felicity, handing her friends pieces of paper and pens. "The first thing to do is write down everything you can see."

"We don't need paper to write that down," grumbled Holly. "There's trees, grass, a pond, flowers, sky, and that's it." She was seriously contemplating going to Sparkles on her own.

Felicity could see she was going to have to work hard to persuade Holly that her party theme was a good idea.

"Perhaps if we just look at one of
those things you mentioned, you
might see what I mean," she said,
kneeling down. "Let's study my pond."
Reluctantly, her friends knelt
down beside her and looked
deep into the water.
"I didn't know you had
goldfish!" said Daisy,

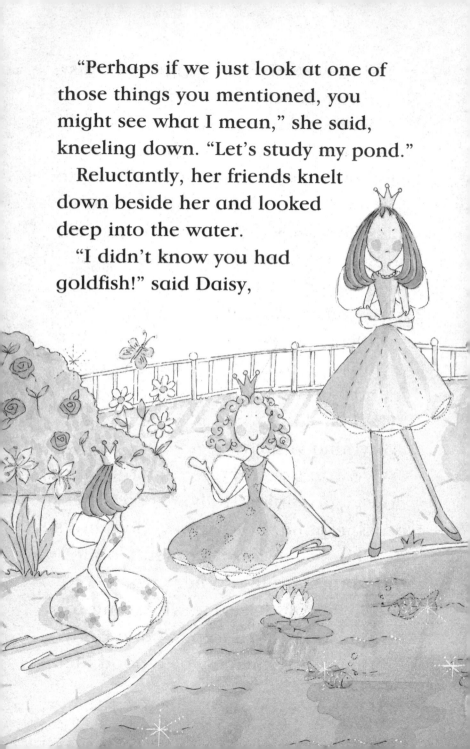

squealing and pointing to a flash of
orange that quickly disappeared
under a leaf.

"I love the colour of goldfish," said
Holly, suddenly paying attention.
"Sometimes when the sunlight catches
the surface of the water they almost
look like they're made
of real gold."

Felicity grinned. "Well, perhaps you could make an outfit like that for the party?" she suggested.

"Come as a fish?" said a shocked Holly. "I don't think so."

"No, silly!" said Felicity, giggling. "Make a beautiful golden-orange dress that shimmers like the scales of a goldfish. You could even add a fishtail to it."

Holly was in raptures. For the first time since Felicity had given out the invitations she was getting excited about the party.

"Oh, I want to be a goldfish now too!" said Polly, admiring Holly's sketch of her party outfit.

"Me too!" said Daisy.

"Well, there are plenty of other things you could go as," said Felicity. "Let's write down everything we see in my garden and then we can choose what we're going to create over a hot chocolate at Sparkles!"

✳ ✳ ✳

For the next few hours Felicity, Daisy, Polly, and even Holly studied the nature in Felicity's garden inch by inch. Even when they'd filled both sides of their paper, there were still more things to write. The list was endless.

Ladybirds   Clouds
Raindrop   Leaves
Spiderwebs   Butterflies
Grass   Petals
Buttercup   Buds
Sky   Caterpillars
Birds   Blackberries
Clover   Redcurrants
Feathers   Rosehip
Sunshine   Snails

"I'd really like to come as a flower," said Daisy, setting down her hot chocolate on the coffee table, "but I just don't know which one."

"A poppy?" suggested Holly, whose favourite colour was red.

"A daisy!" said Polly. "Just like your name!"

"Why don't you come as them all?" said Felicity. "We could sew some real flowers on to your tights."

"I've got a flowery bag and flowery earrings you could borrow!" said Holly.

"And you could hold a big bouquet of flowers too!" joined in Polly.

"Hmm," said Daisy, unconvinced. "It's a nice idea but I think I might end up looking a bit of a fright, covered head to toe in flowers!"

"Then what about a posy?" suggested Felicity. "I've got a lovely green dress you could wear. You'd only need to get some green tights and shoes."

"What, and hold a flower posy in my hands?" asked Daisy.

"Well you *could*," said Felicity, "but the fun of fancy dress is that you wear something you'd never usually wear. I've just thought of something – you could put all your favourite flowers in your hair!"

"I think it's a great idea!" said Holly, who loved experimenting with hairstyles.

"You'll look beautiful!" said Polly. "But what am I going to go as? I've got plenty of ideas but none of them

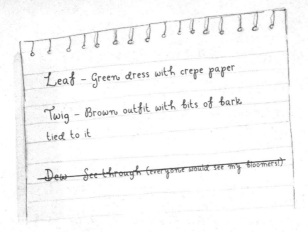

Leaf - Green dress with crepe paper

Twig - Brown outfit with bits of bark tied to it

~~Dew - See-through~~ (everyone would see my bloomers!)

seem special enough."

"I think it's time to let shopping be our inspiration for nature!" said Felicity. "You never know, you might just see one thing, like a fantastic black and yellow jumper, and decide you're going to go to the party as a bumblebee!"

"Is that what you're going to do?" asked Polly.

Felicity suddenly looked very secretive.

"Maybe!" she said, tapping her nose with her wand. "That would be telling!"

With much excitement, the fairy friends gathered up their things and headed into town.

First stop was the bead shop in Little Blossoming. It sold far more than its name suggested. You could find buttons, bows, sequins, stickers, glitter, thread and even rare gems to make anything ordinary suddenly special.

Felicity, Holly, Polly and Daisy decided to split up to scour the shop for ideas.

Daisy was choosing ribbon for her posy outfit. Holly had found some shimmering orange sequins for her fishtail dress. Polly was buried in an amazing assortment of silks and netting that would form the wings of a stunning butterfly outfit. And Felicity was in the basement, pointing out which sparkling gems she'd like.

"Gorgeous, aren't they?" said
Felicity to the tall fairy waiting in the
queue behind her. "I've spent days

searching for the right gems for my party outfit. I had almost given up hope, when I saw these sky-blue sapphires glittering in the shop window."

"Yes, they are lovely," said the tall fairy, admiring them.

"I'm sorry to keep you waiting so long," said the fairy assistant, polishing the last of Felicity's gems. "I've almost finished."

"Please don't worry," said the tall fairy politely. "Just as long as you leave some of the sky-blue sapphires for me."

"I'm afraid this young fairy has just had the last dozen," said the assistant. "The next delivery comes in two weeks, if you'd like me to put some by for you."

"Oh dear!" cried the fairy. "That's far too late. I need them now."

Felicity felt terrible. It was in her

nature to share but she'd spent ages
choosing the perfect gems to make
her outfit really sparkle, and couldn't
bear to start the search again.

"Usually I'd offer them to you,"
said Felicity reluctantly, "but I'm
afraid I really need them; none of
the others would be right for my
outfit."

"I don't know what I'm going to do
now," said the fairy, visibly upset.

Felicity thought for a while. "I
don't need them until next Saturday,
when I'm having a party. If you like,
you could borrow them until then?"

Instead of smiling, as Felicity had
hoped, the fairy looked even more
unhappy. Trying to remain
composed she replied, "Thank you,
but I need them for a party next
Saturday too."

"Are you absolutely sure that you
have nothing else that's similar in

colour and just as stunning?" said
Felicity, turning to the assistant with
a hopeful look.

The assistant slowly shook her head.
"I'm afraid not."

"Then these are for you," said
Felicity, holding the sapphires out to
the tall fairy. "Having all my fairy
friends at the party will provide more
than enough sparkle. Take these as a
present."

The tall fairy's face suddenly lit up.
"Thank you, thank you. You don't
know how much this means to me,"
she said, giving Felicity a big hug.

Felicity was disappointed for herself
but delighted that she had made
another fairy so happy. With a warm
glow she fluttered off to find Holly,
Polly and Daisy.

* * *

"Look what I found!" beamed Polly,
wiggling a bag full of shimmering

silks and netting in front of Felicity's
nose.

Felicity sighed.

"Polly's decided she's going to be a
butterfly!" said Holly and Daisy
together.

"That's as long as it's not what
you've chosen to be," said Polly to
Felicity, noticing that her friend
seemed a little unhappy.

"I don't know what I'm going to
be any more," said Felicity, sadly. "I

can't be what I had planned without finding something I can sew on to my outfit that's sky blue and very twinkly. Maybe I should just wear my plain pink dress and go as a strawberry?"

"No, that's far too boring," said Holly. "You were the one that said we had to use our imaginations more!"

"But I don't have any better ideas," said Felicity, feeling a little teary.

"Well, you could always use this!" said Holly, Polly and Daisy together, unwrapping a dazzling sky-blue sapphire gem necklace and handing it to Felicity.

Felicity gasped. "Wow! It's even more beautiful than the sapphires I found here. Where did you get it from?"

"While you were busy downstairs with the assistant, we nipped across to the jewellery shop to find you something to say thank you for all your help in finding our dream party outfits. We couldn't have done it without you, Felicity," said Daisy.

Felicity beamed; not because her fancy dress outfit was now complete, but because she had the best friends in the whole of Fairy World.

Party Pickle

The day of Felicity Wishes' fancy dress party had finally arrived.

All morning Felicity and her friends, Holly, Polly and Daisy, had been decorating the house with baby-pink streamers, cerise balloons and cherry-pink banners. Dressing Felicity's house for a party was normally exciting enough, but this time the four fairy friends had the added thrill of dressing themselves just as flamboyantly!

For the last week the fairy friends had spent every spare moment they had adding the final touches to their fantastic fancy dress outfits. Sequins, buttons, ribbons and glitter covered each of their bedroom floors.

"Wow!" chorused Felicity, Holly and Daisy when they saw Polly's amazing outfit for the first time.

"Do you think it's OK?" asked Polly, opening the box fully.

"OK?" said Holly incredulously. "It's fantastic! You're bound to win the prize for the best outfit."

"Put it on!" urged Felicity.

"No," teased Polly. "You will have to wait until this afternoon like everyone else."

"Oh, go on. You could give us a sneak preview," encouraged Holly, desperate to see the full effect of Polly's outfit.

Polly looked at her watch. "Later! Look, we've only got two more hours before everyone will start arriving and I've still got a batch of brownies to put in the oven!"

Felicity gulped. Two hours wasn't long and there was still so much to do... including putting the finishing touches to her own outfit.

She was almost sure there was something else she had to do as well, something very important, but for the moment she couldn't remember what it was.

Without losing a moment more, the fairies went back to work. Felicity's house was suddenly humming with frantically flapping wings as floors were swept, tables were laid, cakes were iced, and a grand stage was made for the winner of the best fancy dress costume.

* * *

"Phew! I think that's it!" said Holly, puffing her cheeks out and admiring their hard work. "I don't know about you three, but I'm going to start getting ready. Bagsy the bathroom first, and no peeking until I'm transformed!" With that, she was off.

"You two can use the spare bedroom to get changed if you like," offered Felicity to Polly and Daisy. "I've still got a couple of last-minute tweaks to my outfit."

Felicity started up the stairs to her bedroom and then leaned over the banister to call back to Polly and Daisy: "If I'm not down by the time the first guest arrives, please could you let them in for me?"

* * *

Holly had barely finished doing her hair when she heard Felicity's doorbell chime.

"I'll get it!" she called out to the others, who were still getting ready.

"Hello!" welcomed Holly loudly as she opened the door to the most enormous snowflake she had ever seen. "What an incredible outfit!"

Holly tried to work out who was under all the twinkling white snow.

"Are you going to let me in then, Felicity?" said the fairy, giggling under her mask. Holly stepped back to allow the snowflake through the door. "I'm not Felicity, I'm Holly!" she said, pulling off her orange head-dress.

"Holly!" exclaimed the fairy. "You look fantastic! I had no idea it was you behind that mask!"

The theme for Felicity's fancy dress party was nature. And after much thought and deliberation, Holly had transformed a very plain orange dress into a figure-hugging, shimmering vision crowned with a glittering tangerine head-dress.

"And I've got no idea who you are!" said Holly, looking for clues.

"Oh, how can you not know who it is!" giggled Floella the Frost Fairy.

"My outfit gives it away!" But before Holly had a chance to guess, the doorbell went again.

When she opened the door this time, she was greeted by an enormous caterpillar!

"Hello, Felicity!" said two voices at once, one from the front and one from the back of the costume.

"Hello! Hello!" said Holly, giggling. She was about to explain that she wasn't Felicity, but found herself greeting more guests instead!

* * *

By the time Polly and Daisy came downstairs, the whole house was full of fairies dressed up as every element of nature you could ever imagine. There were flower outfits, ladybird dresses, sunshine sunglasses and raindrop hats.

"Doesn't Felicity look great in that goldfish outfit?" said a fairy in a fluffy white cloud costume to Polly.

"Is that Felicity?" asked Polly, pouring herself a large glass of rainbow juice. "I thought *Holly* was coming as a goldfish, but perhaps they swapped their outfits at the last minute."

"Unless that's Holly over there," said Daisy, who had overheard their conversation and had spotted another goldfish on the other side of the room.

"Oh goodness!" said Polly, giggling. "No one knows who anyone is!"

"Guessing who has come as what is all part of the fun of a fancy dress party!" said the cloud.

"I bet I can guess who you are!" said Daisy, giving the cloud a tiny squeeze. "I saw you having a nap in the chair in the corner earlier, Tilly!"

Tilly giggled. She had wanted to be a Dream Fairy for as long as she could remember. Coming to a fancy dress party as a cloud was a natural choice.

"I'm worried that Felicity isn't here," said Polly quietly to Daisy, once they were alone. "That goldfish is definitely Holly – I can tell by the way she swishes her head-dress."

"I think you're right," said Daisy. "The other goldfish fairy is Stella from my Maths class. See, some of her long dark hair has escaped from under her glittery cap."

"Let's go on a mission to find Felicity then!" announced Polly, finishing her juice. "I'll meet you back here in ten minutes!"

✳ ✳ ✳

The whole of the ground floor was packed. Daisy and Polly had enough

trouble squeezing through each of the rooms, let alone trying to find Felicity, in the sea of amazing and hilarious outfits.

When they met back at the drinks table both of them were ninety-nine per cent sure that they'd seen Felicity standing alone by the front door, holding a large golden envelope.

"There were just too many fairies to flutter through to get close enough to check," said Polly, relieved to have found a bit of space.

"I know," agreed Daisy. "My flowery hair-do kept getting in the way, and I knew I'd never make it past that enormous, blue-feathered bird costume."

Daisy wanted to be a Blossom Fairy one day and had come to the party as a posy of her favourite flowers.

"It must have been her though!" said Polly, convinced. "It is by far the most beautiful outfit at the whole party. Coming as a peacock is just perfect for someone as colourful as Felicity."

"It's definitely Felicity. The golden envelope she's holding must be the prize for the best outfit."

"There's one thing that doesn't make sense though," said Polly, looking puzzled. "It's very unlike Felicity to stand alone at her own party."

"Who's alone?" boomed a blaze of colour that bounced in front of them so quickly that it took up their whole field of vision.

"Felicity's alone," said Polly and Daisy, taken aback by the enormous rainbow that stood before them. "She's standing by the front door, probably pondering the best outfit for the competition," said Polly. "And if I were you, I'd head right over there

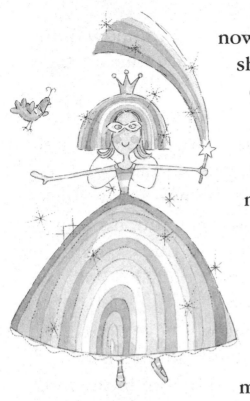

now," said Daisy, shielding her eyes from the rainbow's brilliance. "I think you may just win!"

"I can't win my own competition!" said the rainbow, laughing. "It's me under here!"

Polly and Daisy looked confused.

"Me! Felicity!" The rainbow lifted her enormous coloured skirt to reveal a pair of Felicity's trademark stripy tights.

"Sorry I'm late joining the party. I had to add a few final touches to my outfit. Those sky-blue sapphire stones that you gave me are just perfect."

Felicity shimmied her rainbow outfit to show off the intense colour of the gems.

"If you're here, then I wonder who that is by the door? We thought you'd come as a peacock!" said Daisy.

"Felicity, this is the best party ever! I've never had so much fun. No one knows who anyone is, and everyone else thinks you're a goldfish!" Polly said with a laugh.

"At least no one will have noticed my late arrival then!" said Felicity and she skipped off to join in the fun.

* * *

The fancy dress party went on all afternoon.

Fairies dressed as ladybirds, grasshoppers, blackberries and exotic flowers danced, ate and played games until finally it was time for Felicity to announce the winner of the best outfit.

"It's been a very tough decision,"

confided Felicity to her friends.

"Iona has my vote," said Daisy. "She looks amazing in her blue-feathered bird outfit."

"Eliza has to win," said Holly, swishing her goldfish tail. "It took her days to sew each of those blue beads on to her outfit to make such a wonderful waterfall."

"I think it has to be the peacock with the golden envelope," said Polly, pointing to the fairy who was no longer standing alone, but dancing in the centre of a circle of fairies while she spun and twisted to the music.

"Yes," said Felicity. "I think you're

right. Her outfit is so detailed it looks as though it's been professionally made."

"I think one of the best things about it," mused Polly, "is that it's the only outfit that still has us guessing who is underneath!"

"We have a winner then!" said Felicity, and everyone agreed.

Carefully, Felicity squeezed herself through the partying fairies to reach the stage that she and her friends had built earlier that day.

"Ahem!" she coughed, clearing her throat and waggling her wand for silence. "Thank you all very much for coming. And thank you also for making such a fantastic effort to dress up so brilliantly."

Whoops and cheers filled the room.

"It's been a very hard choice to decide the winner of the prize for best outfit, everyone has created their own individual piece of magic. But finally, after a lot of deliberation, I've decided it should go to the fairy dressed as the peacock!"

A loud round of applause filled the room as all eyes turned to the peacock fairy who was reluctantly being pushed to the stage to collect her prize.

Suddenly Felicity looked panic-stricken. The prize! Felicity had forgotten all about the prize. She'd been so consumed in sewing the sky-blue sapphires on to her rainbow outfit and then so swept up in the party itself that she'd forgotten all about the chocolate cake she'd meant to bake as a prize!

"Thank you!" said the peacock fairy, getting up on the platform. "And

thank you especially to Felicity for
choosing my outfit as the best today."

Everyone cheered. Felicity glanced
round desperately. Tiny beads of
sweat broke out across her brow.

"I'm afraid, though, I will not be
able to accept your prize," the peacock
fairy said. Fairies everywhere looked
bewildered. Felicity raised her
eyebrows in disbelief and then looked
relieved.

"Lots of fairies today have been
trying to guess who I am," continued
the peacock fairy. "And when I take
off my mask you'll understand why I
do not deserve to win."

All the fairies at the party held their
breath.

"Do you think it's Fairy Godmother?"
whispered Holly to Polly. "Maybe she
used some fairy magic to make her
outfit?"

Slowly the peacock fairy undid the

ribbons to her mask as the brightly dressed fairies watched in anticipation.

"You don't know me!" she announced. "I only came to deliver this envelope, but when the door was opened I was swept up in such great waves of fun and friendship I found I just had to stay!"

Surprised fairies clapped and cheered even though they realised that they had no idea who the peacock fairy was.

"I am the lady-in-waiting to a very grand fairy who was helped by Felicity's generous friendship when she let her have her very own sky-blue sapphire stones. It is from this grand fairy that I bring this envelope."

The peacock fairy handed Felicity the golden envelope that she'd been holding throughout the party.

"Open it! Open it!" everyone called.

Slowly Felicity opened the envelope

and took out the glittering card inside. As she read the card a smile lit up her face.

"It's an invitation to a Fairy Masked Ball, tonight, by request of the Grand Fairy of Featherstone!"

"If I had been able to make a wish for myself," continued Felicity, "it would have been for a party that never ended, and in a funny kind of way that secret wish has come true!"

And how all her fancy dressed friends clapped and cheered!

The Grand Fairy of Featherstone
requests the pleasure of
Felicity Wishes
to the Fairy Masked Ball

Being selfless with precious things

will bring rare gems of unexpected happiness

Rapturous Rainbows

If there was one thing that Felicity Wishes loved more than a party, it was a surprise! So she was beside herself with excitement when she was surprised with an invitation to the famous Fairy Masked Ball.

Every year, the Grand Fairy of Featherstone threw an incredible ball to celebrate the end of summer. Felicity had never met Fairy Featherstone but had unknowingly helped her out of a tricky situation recently. It was with grateful thanks for this kindness that Fairy

Featherstone had invited Felicity to her ball.

"Whatever am I going to wear?" exclaimed Felicity to her three fairy friends, Holly, Polly and Daisy, as she dashed around her bedroom, rummaging through drawers and flinging open cupboard doors.

"Well, whatever you wear, you had better be quick about it," said Daisy, peering out of the bedroom window at the golden stretch limousine that had been sent to collect Felicity.

"I've never been to a Fairy Masked Ball before. I don't want to be underdressed but then again I don't want to be overdressed either!" panicked Felicity.

"Why don't you wear what you have got on?" suggested Holly.

Felicity had just finished throwing a fancy dress party and for it she had created a beautiful, vibrant rainbow costume. The skirt and head-dress created a glittering arc that was covered in gems and beads of every colour.

"If you take off the head-dress and just wear a simple mask I think it will be perfect," continued Holly, pulling the head-dress off Felicity's head before she had a chance to respond.

Holly, Polly and Daisy stepped back and looked at Felicity in awe. Felicity turned to look in the mirror.

"Are you sure it's not too over the top?" asked Felicity, swishing from side to side to admire the fullness of her skirt's glorious colours.

"It's perfect," said Holly, smoothing down the creases in the skirt. "I've seen pictures taken at these sorts of balls before and everyone always looks a little overdressed. Remember, you have to stand out to be seen!"

Felicity just didn't feel right. She always preferred to be one of the gang, and standing out from the crowd worried her, especially at a party where she'd know no one at all.

"You'll be fine!" Daisy assured her, reading her friend's mind. "You're the friendliest fairy in the whole of Little Blossoming. People will see the glittering sparkle of your personality way before they see your rainbow skirt!"

"Even so, I think I'd feel more comfortable in this," said Felicity, as she picked up her favourite pink dress.

"Well, put it on underneath!" said Polly, who was always practical. "If you get to the ball and feel out of place then you can slip off your party outfit and wear your pink dress instead."

BEEP! BEEP! BEEP!

"Sounds like I've got to go!" said Felicity nervously, as she quickly slid on her reliable pink dress underneath her party outfit.

"Wish me luck!" she cried, as she very carefully made her way down the stairs.

* * *

Outside she was greeted by Suki, Fairy Featherstone's lady-in-waiting, and shown into the large limousine. Inside, the seats were lined with dusty-pink velvet and huge feather cushions trimmed with golden tassels lay everywhere. Felicity sat back and enjoyed a glass of sparkling pink strawberryade as she was driven along the winding roads of Little Blossoming, towards the ball.

With every corner they turned, the butterflies in Felicity's tummy fluttered more and more.

"Fairy Featherstone is looking forward to meeting you," said Suki, interrupting Felicity's thoughts. "She hasn't stopped talking about your kind friendship since you gave her your sky-blue sapphire gems."

"It was nothing," said Felicity honestly. "Fairy Featherstone seemed to need the gems far more than I did so it only seemed natural to offer them to her."

"I've known Fairy Featherstone a very long time and she is very particular about what she wears."

"I have a friend like that," said Felicity, smiling and thinking of Holly.

"The sky-blue sapphires you gave her were to decorate her crown. Every year Fairy Featherstone chooses a different coloured dress to wear for the ball, and adds a gem of the same colour to her crown."

"So this year Fairy Featherstone will be wearing sky-blue?" asked Felicity.

Suki nodded and giggled. She leaned forward and whispered in Felicity's ear. "It's become very important to Fairy Featherstone that no one else at the Masked Ball wears the same colour as her. It's her party and she always likes to stand out the most."

Felicity looked sheepishly down at her rainbow skirt with its sky-blue sapphires.

"Don't worry about that!" said Suki, noticing the worried look on Felicity's face. "It's really only the main colour that will worry Fairy Featherstone, and as well as sky-blue, *you* are wearing every colour of the rainbow!"

✳ ✳ ✳

At last the limousine arrived at the
gates of a glamorously long drive.

As it wound its way onwards, Felicity stared open-mouthed at the glorious gardens that surrounded the house. Daisy would love this! she thought to herself.

Three pretty fairies were waiting to greet guests on their arrival. They were all dressed identically to Suki, with exquisite peacock feathers and tiny bejewelled masks.

One opened the limousine door, another helped Felicity out and the third fairy curtseyed delicately before offering her a sparkling glass of fruit punch.

Felicity took a deep breath and looked up at the enormous red-carpeted steps that led to the gigantic mansion house in front of her. Feeling a little lost, she looked back for Suki, but she was lost in an intense conversation with another fairy.

Straightening her mask and taking

a deep breath, Felicity began to walk
towards the golden glow of the ball.
The grand entrance hall was
magnificent and unlike anything
Felicity had ever seen before.
Enormous chandeliers glittered with
prisms that showered the walls with
a million rainbows.

It looked as though all the guests had arrived some time ago and the ball was already in full swing. As Felicity approached she no longer worried about standing out. All around her, beautiful fairies hovered, flew and delicately teetered on tiptoe in exquisite clothes.

On the other side of the hall Felicity could see an elegant fairy dressed entirely in sky-blue. She was surrounded by several peacock-feathered helpers.

Fairy Feathersone! thought Felicity to herself as she made her way over to thank her for her kind invitation.

She was just a few steps away when someone bumped into Felicity from behind and made her spill the remainder of her fruit punch all over her beautiful rainbow skirt.

"Oh, I'm terribly sorry," said a familiar voice.

"Don't worry," said Felicity, looking down at her skirt and then up at the fairy, whom she recognised immediately.

"Suki!" she exclaimed. "Honestly, don't worry. You can't see where it spilled because of all the colours. It just needs to dry a bit," she continued cheerfully.

"Oh Felicity, I'm so sorry. I'm afraid there's been a bit of a catastrophe and I wasn't looking where I was going. If you come out the back with me I've got some magic clean-and-dry powder that will have your skirt as good as new in no time."

Suki led Felicity quickly through a series of doors until they reached a small room. It was lined wall to wall with bottles and potions of every description.

"Here it is," she said, reaching up on tiptoe and pulling down a slim

glass tube with a crystal stopper. "If
only all problems were as easy to
solve as this," she said as she carefully
poured out a pinch of powder into
the palm of her hand.

"Have you seen the fairy dressed in
sky-blue?" asked Suki, sprinkling the
dust all over Felicity's rainbow skirt.

"Yes," said Felicity enthusiastically.
"I was just about to go over and say
thank you to Fairy Featherstone for
her kind invitation."

"Oh, that's not Fairy Featherstone!"

said Suki, sighing deeply as she popped the glass tube back on the shelf. "That's Fairy Montague, who's *also* wearing sky-blue tonight, much to the disgust of Fairy Featherstone. She is in her bedroom now and refuses to come down."

"Oh goodness! Poor Fairy Featherstone," said Felicity, looking down at the magic powder that had not only cleaned and dried her skirt but had given it a glittering transformation to make it far brighter than before.

"Goodness indeed!" said Suki, squinting at Felicity's newly cleaned, glittering skirt.

She led Felicity out of the room. "Everyone is supposed to be seated for supper in less than half an hour, which isn't going to happen if Fairy Featherstone is still refusing to come down."

Felicity dragged her mind away from feeling self-conscious in her glowing skirt and thought about Fairy Featherstone.

She tried to imagine how she would have felt if someone else had turned up at her fancy dress party with a similar rainbow outfit. But then again, thought Felicity, surely Fairy Featherstone would have something else to wear more wonderful and eye-catching than any outfit here.

"How many Masked Balls has Fairy Featherstone held?" asked Felicity, as they made their way back along the corridor to the entrance hall.

"This will be the thirtieth," said Suki. "That is why it's so important."

"So Fairy Featherstone's special crown must boast a varied array of thirty different-coloured gems?"

"Yes," said Suki. "She puts a new gem on her crown every year to represent the latest colour. It's so heavy now that this is the only occasion Fairy Featherstone wears it."

"I've got an idea," said Felicity, looking down at her brightly coloured, glittering dress that was now far too over-the-top for her to wear. "Do you think she'd let me help?"

"I think Fairy Featherstone would be pleased to let you help. After all, you helped before!"

It took more persuasion than Suki

had bargained for in order to convince Fairy Featherstone to see Felicity.

Eventually Felicity was ushered into the room and she quickly set about explaining her plan to help Fairy Featherstone stand out the most at her thirtieth Fairy Masked Ball.

* * *

A loud gong sounded three times in the grand entrance hall and a hushed silence fell over the crowd of masked fairies.

Felicity quickly and quietly skipped down the staircase in her pretty pink dress. Pink was her favourite colour and she felt much more at ease in this dress.

"Would everyone please raise their glasses in a toast to welcome our host for this evening's thirtieth Fairy Masked Ball... the Grand Fairy of Featherstone!"

"The Grand Fairy of Featherstone!"

chorused the room, as a vision of
vibrant colour blazed from the top of
the grand staircase.

The entire entrance hall began to
glow with every hue and shade
of the rainbow.

Fairies holding on to their
glasses almost dropped them,

some of those with
ornate masks lifted
them to see if
what they were
seeing was real,
and awe-filled
gasps echoed all
around the room.
Slowly and
carefully, Fairy
Featherstone
descended the
staircase with a
steady, regal air. It
gave all her guests
plenty of time to
appreciate the dazzling
colours that emanated
from her bejewelled crown
and beautiful outfit.

"Thank you all *so*
much for coming!"
announced Fairy

Featherstone, when she reached the bottom.

Her guests broke into rapturous applause.

"As most of you know, each year I celebrate this ball with a new colour. It has been pointed out to me by a new, but very dear, friend that this year's colour, sky-blue, will complete the entire thirty-colour spectrum of our rainbow. Every one of us, in the colours we wear this evening, is part of that rainbow."

Felicity flushed with pride.

"So," continued Fairy Featherstone, "what could be more fitting to celebrate this thirtieth year than a rainbow entrance to welcome you all to this year's Masked Fairy Ball."

Fairy Featherstone gestured to the hundreds of tiny rainbows that shone from the light of the chandeliers on to the walls.

"Please go through to the dining hall. Eat, drink, dance, and above all, have a ball!"

With that everyone clapped and cheered more loudly than ever.

✳ ✳ ✳

The ball went on long into the night and it was agreed by everyone that it had been the best Masked Ball ever.

Fairy Featherstone had been in her element all night. Her outfit had drawn so much attention that it wasn't until Felicity was about to leave that she finally found a chance to speak to her.

"Thank you for inviting me to such a fantastic party!" said Felicity, exhausted by all the fun she'd had. "You know so many lovely fairies – I'm sorry I didn't have time to make friends with them all!"

"Every friend of mine is now a friend of yours, Felicity," said Fairy

Featherstone. "And I know that I have made the most important friend tonight. A rare fairy whose friendship glows with every colour of the rainbow... you!"

There are as many ways
to be a good friend

as there are colours
of the rainbow

If you enjoyed this book, why not try another of these fantastic story collections?

Star Surprise

Designer Drama

Clutter Clean-out

Newspaper Nerves

Enchanted Escape

Whispering Wishes

Friends Forever

Sensational Secrets

Happy Hobbies

Wand Wishes

Party Pickle

Dancing Dreams

13 Spooky Sleepover

14 Fashion Fiasco

15 Pink Paradise

16 Spectacular Skies

17 Dreamy Daisy

18 Perfect Polly

WOULD YOU LIKE TO BE A FRIEND OF FELICITY?

Felicity Wishes has her very own website, filled with lots of sparkly fairy fun and information about Felicity Wishes and all her fairy friends.

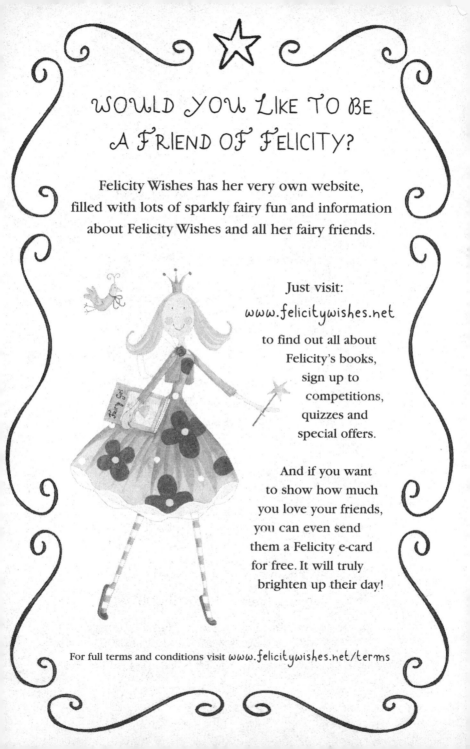

Just visit:

www.felicitywishes.net

to find out all about Felicity's books, sign up to competitions, quizzes and special offers.

And if you want to show how much you love your friends, you can even send them a Felicity e-card for free. It will truly brighten up their day!

For full terms and conditions visit www.felicitywishes.net/terms

SEE YOUR FRIENDSHIP LETTER HERE!

Write in and tell us all about your best friend, and you could see your letter published in one of the Felicity Wishes' books.

Please send in your letter, including your name and age with a stamped self-addressed envelope to:

Felicity Wishes Friendship Competition

Hodder Children's Books, 338 Euston Road, London NW1 3BH

Australian readers should write to...
Hachette Children's Books
Level 17/207 Kent Street, Sydney, NSW 2000, Australia

New Zealand readers should write to...
Hachette Children's Books
PO Box 100-749 North Shore Mail Centre, Auckland, New Zealand

Closing date is 30 April 2007

ALL ENTRIES MUST BE SIGNED BY A PARENT OR GUARDIAN.
TO BE ELIGIBLE ENTRANTS MUST BE UNDER 13 YEARS.

For full terms and conditions visit www.felicitywishes.net/terms